Tucholsky Wagner Zola Scott Sydow Freud Schlegel
Turgenev Fonatne Wallace Walther von der Vogelweide Fouqué Friedrich II. von Preußen
Twain Weber Freiligrath Frey
Fechner Fichte Weiße Rose von Fallersleben Kant Ernst Richthofen Frommel
Engels Fielding Hölderlin Dumas
Fehrs Faber Flaubert Eichendorff Tacitus
Feuerbach Maximilian I. von Habsburg Fock Eliasberg Zweig Ebner Eschenbach
Ewald Eliot Vergil
Goethe Elisabeth von Österreich London
Mendelssohn Balzac Shakespeare Dostojewski Ganghofer
Trackl Lichtenberg Rathenau Doyle Gjellerup
Stevenson Hambruch
Mommsen Tolstoi Lenz Droste-Hülshoff
Thoma Hanrieder
Dach von Arnim Hägele Hauff Humboldt
Karrillon Reuter Verne Rousseau Hagen Hauptmann Gautier
Garschin Defoe Baudelaire
Damaschke Descartes Hebbel
Hegel Kussmaul Herder
Wolfram von Eschenbach Dickens Schopenhauer Rilke George
Bronner Darwin Melville Grimm Jerome
Campe Horváth Aristoteles Bebel Proust
Bismarck Vigny Barlach Voltaire Federer Herodot
Gengenbach Heine
Storm Casanova Tersteegen Grillparzer Georgy
Chamberlain Lessing Langbein Gilm Gryphius
Brentano Lafontaine
Strachwitz Claudius Schiller Kralik Iffland Sokrates
Katharina II. von Rußland Bellamy Schilling
Gerstäcker Raabe Gibbon Tschechow
Löns Hesse Hoffmann Gogol Wilde Vulpius
Luther Heym Hofmannsthal Morgenstern Gleim
Roth Klee Hölty Goedicke
Luxemburg Heyse Klopstock Kleist
Machiavelli La Roche Puschkin Homer Mörike Musil
Navarra Aurel Musset Horaz
Nestroy Marie de France Lamprecht Kind Kirchhoff Kraft Kraus
Laotse Ipsen Hugo Moltke
Nietzsche Nansen Liebknecht
Marx Lassalle Gorki Ringelnatz
von Ossietzky May Klett Leibniz
vom Stein Lawrence Irving
Petalozzi Knigge
Platon Pückler Michelangelo Kock Kafka
Sachs Poe Liebermann Korolenko
de Sade Praetorius Mistral Zetkin

The publishing house tredition has created the series **TREDITION CLASSICS**. It contains classical literature works from over two thousand years. Most of these titles have been out of print and off the bookstore shelves for decades.

The book series is intended to preserve the cultural legacy and to promote the timeless works of classical literature. As a reader of a **TREDITION CLASSICS** book, the reader supports the mission to save many of the amazing works of world literature from oblivion.

The symbol of **TREDITION CLASSICS** is Johannes Gutenberg (1400 – 1468), the inventor of movable type printing.

With the series, tredition intends to make thousands of international literature classics available in printed format again – worldwide.

All books are available at book retailers worldwide in paperback and in hardcover. For more information please visit: www.tredition.com

tredition was established in 2006 by Sandra Latusseck and Soenke Schulz. Based in Hamburg, Germany, tredition offers publishing solutions to authors and publishing houses, combined with worldwide distribution of printed and digital book content. tredition is uniquely positioned to enable authors and publishing houses to create books on their own terms and without conventional manufacturing risks.

For more information please visit: www.tredition.com

The Threshold Grace

Percy C. Ainsworth

Imprint

This book is part of the TREDITION CLASSICS series.

Author: Percy C. Ainsworth
Cover design: toepferschumann, Berlin (Germany)

Publisher: tredition GmbH, Hamburg (Germany)
ISBN: 978-3-8491-4722-8

www.tredition.com
www.tredition.de

Copyright:
The content of this book is sourced from the public domain.

The intention of the TREDITION CLASSICS series is to make world literature in the public domain available in printed format. Literary enthusiasts and organizations worldwide have scanned and digitally edited the original texts. tredition has subsequently formatted and redesigned the content into a modern reading layout. Therefore, we cannot guarantee the exact reproduction of the original format of a particular historic edition. Please also note that no modifications have been made to the spelling, therefore it may differ from the orthography used today.

PREFATORY NOTE

During his brief ministry Mr. Ainsworth published a series of meditations in the columns of the *Methodist Times*, which are here reprinted by the kind permission of the Editor, Dr. Scott Lidgett. The rare interest aroused by the previous publication of Mr. Ainsworth's sermons encourages the hope that the present volume may find a place in the devotional literature to which many turn in the quiet hour.

A.K.S.

CONTENTS

I.

THE THRESHOLD GRACE

The Lord shall keep thy going out and thy coming in, from this time forth and for evermore.

Ps. cxxi, 8.

Going out and coming in. That is a picture of life. Beneath this old Hebrew phrase there lurks a symbolism that covers our whole experience. But let us just now look at the most literal, and by no means the least true, interpretation of these words. One of the great dividing-lines in human life is the threshold-line. On one side of this line a man has his 'world within the world,' the sanctuary of love, the sheltered place of peace, the scene of life's most personal, sacred, and exclusive obligations. And on the other side lies the larger life of mankind wherein also a man must take his place and do his work. Life is spent in crossing this threshold-line, going out to the many and coming in to the few, going out to answer the call of labour and coming in to take the right to rest. And over us all every hour there watches the Almighty Love. The division-lines in the life of man have nothing that corresponds to them in the love of God. We may be here or there, but He is everywhere.

The Lord shall keep thy going out. Life has always needed that promise. There is a pledge of help for men as they fare forth to the world's work. It was much for the folk of an early time to say that as they went forth the Lord went with them, but it is more for men to say and know that same thing to-day. The *going out* has come to mean more age after age, generation after generation. It was a simpler thing once than it is now. 'Thy going out' — the shepherd to his flocks, the farmer to his field, the merchant to his merchandise. There are still flocks and fields and markets, but where are the leisure, grace, and simplicity of life for him who has any share in the world's work? Men go out to-day to face a life shadowed by vast industrial, commercial, and social problems. Life has grown complicated, involved, hard to understand, difficult to deal with. Tension, conflict, subtlety, surprise, and amid it all, or over it all, a vast brooding weariness that ever and again turns the heart sick. Oh the pains and the perils of the going out! There are elements of danger in modern life that threaten all the world's toilers, whatever their work may be and wherever they may have to do it. There is the danger that always lurks in *things*—a warped judgement, a confused reckoning, a narrowed outlook. It is so easily possible for a man to be at close grips with the world and yet to be ever more and more out of touch with its realities. The danger in the places where men toil is not that God is denied with a vociferous atheism; it is that He is ignored by an unvoiced indifference. It is not the babel of the market-place that men need to fear; it is its silence. If we say that we live only as we love, that we are strong only as we are pure, that we are successful only as we become just and good, the world into which we go forth does not deny these things—but it ignores them. And thus the real battle of life is not the toil for bread. It is fought by all who would keep alive and fresh in their hearts the truth that man doth not live by bread alone. For no man is this going out easy, for some it is at times terrible, for all it means a need that only this promise avails to meet—'The Lord shall keep thy going out.' He shall fence thee about with the ministry of His Spirit, and give thee grace to know, everywhere and always, that thou art in this world to live for His kingdom of love and truth and to grow a soul.

The Lord, shall keep ... thy coming in. It might seem to some that once a man was safely across the threshold of his home he might stand in less need of this promise of help. But experience says otherwise. The world has little respect for any man's threshold. It is capable of many a bold and shameless intrusion. The things that harass a man as he earns his tread sometimes haunt him as he eats it. No home is safe unless faith be the doorkeeper. 'In peace will I both lay me down and sleep, for Thou, Lord, alone makest me to dwell in safety.' The singer of that song knew that, as in the moil of the world, so also in the shelter of the place he named his dwelling-place, peace and safety were not of his making, but of God's giving.

Sometimes there is a problem and a pain waiting for a man across his own threshold. Many a man can more easily look upon the difficulties and perils of the outer world than he can come in and look into the pain-lined face of his little child. If we cannot face alone the hostilities on one side of our threshold we cannot face alone the intimacies on the other side of it. After all, life is whole and continuous. Whatever the changes in the setting of life, there is no respite from living. And that means there is no leisure from duty, no rest from the service of obedience, no cessation in the working of all those forces by means of which, or in spite of which, life is ever being fashioned and fulfilled.

And now let us free our minds from the literalism of this promise and get a glimpse of its deeper application to our lives. The threshold of the home does not draw the truest division-line in life between the outward and the inward. Life is made up of thought and action, of the manifest things and the hidden things.

'Thy going out.' That is, our life as it is manifest to others, as it has points of contact with the world about us. We must go out. We must take up some attitude toward all other life. We must add our word to the long human story and our touch to the fashioning of the world. We need the pledge of divine help in that life of ours in which, for their good or ill, others must have a place and a part. 'And thy coming in'—into that uninvaded sanctum of thought. Did we say uninvaded? Not so. In that inner room of life there sits Regret with her pale face, and Shame with dust on her forehead, and Memory with tears in her eyes. It is a pitiable thing at times, is this our coming in. More than one man has consumed his life in a flame of activity because he could not abide the coming in. 'The Lord shall keep … thy coming in.' That means help for every lonely, impotent, inward hour of life.

Look at the last word of this promise—'for evermore.' Going out and coming in for evermore. I do not know how these words were interpreted when very literal meanings were attached to the parabolic words about the streets of gold and the endless song. But they present no difficulty to us. Indeed, they confirm that view of the future which is ever taking firmer hold of men's minds, and which is based on the growing sense of the continuity of life. To offer a man an eternity of music-laden rest is to offer him a poor thing. He would rather have his going out and his coming in. Yes, and he shall have them. All that is purest and best in them shall remain.

Hereafter he shall still go out to find deeper joys of living and wider visions of life; still come in to greater and ever greater thoughts of God.

II.

THE HABIT OF FAITH

Trust in Him at all times, ye people.
Pour out your heart before Him.
God is a refuge for us.

Ps. lxii. 8.

Here the Psalmist strikes the great note of faith as it should be struck. He sets it ringing alike through the hours and the years. *Trust in Him at all times.* Faith is not an act, but an attitude; not an event, but a principle; not a last resource, but the first and abiding necessity. It is the constant factor in life's spiritual reckonings. It is the ever-applicable and the ever-necessary. It is always in the high and lasting fitness of things. There are words that belong to hours or even moments, words that win their meaning from the newly created situation. But faith is not such a word. It stands for something inclusive and imperial. It is one of the few timeless words in earth's vocabulary. For the deep roots of it and the wide range of it there is nothing like unto it in the whole sweep of things spiritual. So the 'all times' trust is not for one moment to be regarded as some supreme degree of faith unto which one here and there may attain and which the rest can well afford to look upon as a counsel of perfection. This exhortation to trust in God at all times concerns first of all the *nature* of faith and not the *measure* of it. All real faith has the note of the eternal in it. It can meet the present because it is not of the present. We have grown familiar with the phrase, 'The man of the moment.' But who is this man? Sometimes he is very literally a man of the moment—an opportunist, a gambler with the hours, a follower of the main chance. The moment makes him, and passing away unmakes him. But the true man of the moment is the man to whom the moment is but one throb in the pulse of eternity. For him the moment does not stand out in splendid isolation. It is set in its place between that which hath been and that which shall be. And its true significance is not something abiding in it, but something running through it. So is it in this great matter of faith. Only the faith that can trust at all times can trust at any time. The moment that faith heeds the dictation of circumstance it ceases to be faith and becomes calculation. All faith is transcendent. It is independent of the conditions in which it has to live. It is not snared in the strange web of the tentative and the experimental. He that has for one moment felt the power of faith has got beyond the dominion of time.

Trust in Him at all times. That is the only real escape from confusion and contradiction in the judgements we are compelled to pass upon life. Times change so suddenly and inexplicably. The hours seem to be at strife with each other. We live in the midst of a perpetual conflict between our yesterdays and our to-days. There is no simple, obvious sequence in the message of experience. The days will not dovetail into each other. Life is compact of much that is impossible of true adjustment at the hands of any time-born philosophy. And in all this seeming confusion there lies the necessity for faith. Herein it wins its victory. We are to trust God not because we cannot trace Him, but that by trusting Him we may ever be more able to trace Him and to see that He has a way through all these winding and crossing paths. Faith does more than hold a man's hand in the darkness; it leads him into the light. It is the secret of coherence and harmony. It does not make experience merely bearable, it makes it luminous and instructive. It takes the separate or the tangled strands of human experience and weaves them into one strong cable of help and hope.

Trust in Him at all times. Then faith at its best is a habit. Indeed, religion at its best is a habit, too! We are sometimes too ready to discount the worth of the habitual in our religious life. We put a premium on self-consciousness. We reduce the life of faith to a series of acts of faith of varying difficulty and import, but each detached from the rest and individually apprehended of the soul. Surely this is all wrong. In our physical life we are least conscious of those functions that are most vital and continuous, and the more perfectly they do their work the less we think about them. The analogy is incomplete and must be drawn with care. But when you have con-

ceded that faith has to be acquired, that it has to be learned, there is
still this much in the analogy. If faith is a long and hard lesson, the
value of the lesson to us is not the effort with which we learn it, but
the ease with which we apply it. The measure of conscious effort in
our faith is the measure of our faith's weakness. When faith has
become a spontaneity of our character, when it turns to God instinc-
tively, when it does its work with the involuntariness of habit, then
it has become strong.

Pour out your heart before Him. How this singer understood the office and privilege of the 'all times' trust! He knew that there is a
fullness of heart that is ill to bear. True, in more than one simple
way the full heart can find some slight relief. There is work. The full
heart can go out and do something. There is a brother's trouble in
which a man may partly forget his own. There is sympathy. Surely
few are so lonely that they cannot find any one ready to offer the
gift of the listening ear, any one willing to share with them all of
pain and burden that can be shared. Ah! but what of that which
cannot be shared? What of the sorrow that has no language, and the
shame and confusion that we would not, and even dare not, trail
across a friend's mind? So often the heart holds more than ever
should be poured out into another's ear. There are in life strained
silences that we could not break if we would. And there is a law of
reticence that true love and unselfishness will always respect. If my
brother hath joy, am I to cloud it with my grief? If he hath sorrow,
am I to add my sorrow unto his? When our precious earthly fellowship has been put to its last high uses in the hour of sorrow or
shame, the heart has still a burden for which this world finds no
relief. But there is another fellowship. There is God our Father.
There is the ear of Heaven. We may be girt with silence among our
fellows, but in looking up the heart finds freedom. In His Presence
the voice of confession can break through the gag of shame, and the
pent-up tide of trouble can let itself break upon the heart of Eternal
Love.

God is a refuge for us. That is the great discovery of faith. That is
the merciful word that comes to be written so plainly in the life that
has formed the habit of faith. God our refuge. It may be that to some
the word 'refuge' suggests the occasional rather than the constant
need of life. But the refuge some day and the faith every day are

linked together. A thing is no use to you if you cannot find it when you want it. And you cannot find it easily if it be not at hand. The peasant built his cottage under the shadow of his lord's castle walls. In the hour of peril it was but a step to the strong fortress. 'Trust in Him at all times.' Build your house under the walls of the Eternal Help. Live in the Presence. Find the attitude of faith, and the act of faith will be simple. Trust in Him through every hour, and when a tragic hour comes one step shall take you into the innermost safety.

III.

THE ONE THING DESIRABLE

One thing have I desired of the Lord, that will I seek after; that I may dwell in the house of the Lord all the days of my life, to behold the beauty of the Lord, and to inquire in His temple.

Ps. xxvii. 4.

I have desired … I will seek. Amid the things that are seen, desire and quest are nearly always linked closely together. The man who desires money seeks after money. The desire of the world is often disappointed, but it is rarely supine. It is dynamic. It leads men. True, it leads them astray; but that is a reflection on its wisdom and not on its effectiveness. Among what we rightly call the lower things men do not play with their desires, they obey them. But amid the unseen realities of life it is often quite otherwise. In the religious life desire is sometimes strangely ineffective. It is static, if that be not a contradiction in terms. In many a life-story it stands written: One thing have I desired of the Lord, that will I dream of, that will I hope for, that will I wait for. Many things help to explain this attitude, and, explaining it, they condemn it also. We allow our surroundings to pass judgement on our longings. We bring the eternal to the bar of the hour, and postpone the verdict. Or it may be in the worldliness of our hearts we admit the false plea of urgency and the false claim of authority made by our outward life. And perhaps more commonly the soul lacks the courage of its desires. It costs little to follow a desire that goes but a little way, and that on the level of familiar effort and within sight of familiar things. It is another thing to hear the call of the mountains and to feel the fascination of some far and glittering peak. That is a call to perilous and painful effort. And yet again, high desire sometimes leaves life where it found it because the heart attaches an intrinsic value to vision. It is something to have *seen* the Alpine heights of possibility. Yes, it is something, but what is it? It is a golden hour to the man who sets out to the climb; it is an hour of shame and judgement, hereafter to be manifest, to the man who clings to the comforts of the valley.

One thing have I desired. When a man speaks thus unto us, we have a right to ponder his words with care. We naturally become profoundly interested, expectant, and, to the limit of our powers, critical. If a man has seen one thing that he can call simply and finally the desire of his heart, it ought to be worth looking at. We expect something large, lofty, inclusive. And we find this: *'That I may dwell in the house of the Lord all the days of my life, to behold the beauty of the Lord, and to inquire in His temple.'* Let us examine this desire, And, first of all, we must free our minds from mere literalism. If we do not, we shall find in this desire many things that are not in it, and miss everything that is in it. This is not the longing for a cloistered life, the confession of one who is weary of this heavy world, doubtful of its promises and afraid of its powers. 'The house of the Lord' is not a place, but a state, not an edifice, but an attitude. It is a fair and unseen dwelling-place builded by the hands of God to be the home, here and hereafter, of all the hearts that purely love and worship Him. We read of one who, a day's march from his father's house, lay down and slept; and in his sleep God spake to him, and lo, out in a wild and lonely place, Jacob said, 'This is none other but the house of God.' For every one to whom the voice of God has come, and who has listened to that voice and believed in its message, the mountains and valleys of this fair world, the breath of every morning and the hush of every evening, are instinct with a Presence. Wordsworth dwelt in the house of the Lord all the days of his life. And if the wonder and beauty of the earth lift up our hearts unto our God in praise and worship, we dwell there also.

Yes, but this world is a world of men. In city or on hillside the great persistent fact for us, the real setting of our life, is not nature, but humanity. Life is not a peaceful vision of earthly beauty. Our experience is not a dreamy pastoral. There are shamed and broken lives. The world is full of greed and hate and warfare and sorrow. Nature at its best cannot by itself build for us a temple that humanity at its worst, or even at something less than its worst, cannot pull down about our ears. For the Psalmist, probably David himself, the temple was symbolic of all heavenly realities. It stood for the holiness and the nearness and the mercy of God, and for the sacredness and the possibility of human life. In the light and power and perfect assurance of these things he desired to dwell all the days of his life. For us there is the life and word of One greater than the temple. Jesus of Nazareth dwelt in the house of the Lord. Between Him and God the Father there was perfect union. And no one ever saw the worth of human life as Jesus saw it. And no one ever measured the sacred values of humanity as He measured them. And now, in the perfect mercy of God, there is no man but may dwell in the house of God alway and feel life's sacredness amidst a thousand desecrations, and know its preciousness amidst all that seeks to obscure, defile, and cheapen it.

To behold the beauty of the Lord. It is only in the house of the Lord, the unseen fane of reverence, trust, and communion, that a man can learn what beauty is, and where to look for it. Out in the world beauty is held to be a sporadic thing. It is like a flower growing where no one expected a blossom. It is an unrelated and unexplained surprise. It is a green oasis in the desert of unlovely and unpromising things. But for the dweller in the house of the Lord beauty is not on this wise. Said one such dweller, 'The desert shall rejoice and blossom as the rose.' He looked across the leagues of burning sand and saw the loveliness of Carmel by the sea, and of Sharon where the lilies grow. To the artist beauty is an incident, to the saint beauty is a law of life. It is the thing that is to be. It is the positive purpose, throbbing and yearning and struggling in the whole universe. When it emerges and men behold it, they behold the face of truth; and if it emerges not, it is still there, the fundamental fact and the vital issue of human life. To dwell in the Divine Presence by faith and obedience; to live so near to God that you can see all about yourself and every human soul the real means of life, and straight before you the real end of life; to know that though so often the worst is man's dark choice, yet ever the best is his true heritage; and to learn to interpret the whole of life in the terms of God's saving purpose,—this is to behold the beauty of the Lord.

And to inquire in His temple. The Psalmist desired for himself an inward attitude before God that should not only reveal unto him the eternal fitness of all God's ways and the eternal grace of all His purposes, but should also put him in the way of solving the various problems that arise to try the wisdom and strength of men's lives. Sometimes the first court of appeal in life, and always the last, is the temple court. When all the world is dumb, a voice speaks to them that worship. Reverential love never loses its bearings. In this world we need personal and social guidance, and there must be many times when both shall be wanting unless we have learned to carry the burden of our ignorance to the feet of the Eternal Wisdom. And perhaps a man can desire no better thing for himself than that the reverence and devotion of his life should be such as to make the appeal to God's perfect arbitrament an easy thing.

IV.

EYES AND FEET

Mine eyes are ever toward the Lord,
For He shall pluck my feet out of the net.

Ps. xxv. 15.

In any man's life a great deal depends upon outlook. In some
ways we recognize this fact. We do not by choice live in a house
whose windows front a blank wall. A little patch of green grass, a
tree, a peep of sky, or even the traffic of a busy street—anything
rather than a blank wall. That is a sound instinct, but it ought to go
deeper than it sometimes does. This outlook and aspect question is
important when you are building a house, but it is vastly more important when you are building a character. The soul has eyes. The
deadliest monotony is that of a dull soul. Life is a poor affair for any
man who looks out upon the blind walls of earthly circumstance
and necessity, and cannot see from his soul's dwelling-place the
pink flush of the dawn that men call hope, and who has no garden
where he may grow the blossoms of faith and sweet memory, the
fair flowers of holy human trusts and fellowships. Only the divinity
of life can deliver us from the monotony of living. 'Mine eyes are
ever toward the Lord.' This man has an infinite outlook. It matters
not whether he looked out through palace windows or lived in the
meanest house in Jerusalem's city. It is the eye that makes the view.
This man had a fairer prospect than ever man had who looked sea-
ward from Carmel or across the valleys from the steeps of Libanus.
It was his soul that claimed the prospect. From the window of the
little house of life he saw the light of God lying on the everlasting
hills. That is the real deliverance from the monotony of things. The
man who is weary of life is the man who has not seen it. The man
who is tied to his desk sometimes thinks everything would be right

if only he could travel. But many a man has done the Grand Tour and come back no better contented. You cannot fool your soul with Mont Blanc or even the Himalayas. So many thousand feet, did you say?—but what is that to infinity! The cure for the fretful soul is not to go *round* the world; it is to get *beyond* it.

Mine eyes are ever toward the Lord. That is the view we want. We gaze contemptuously on the little one-story lodge just inside the park gates, and fail to get a glimpse of the magnificent mansion, with its wealth of adornment and treasure, that lies a mile among the trees. No wonder that men grow discontented or contemptuous when they mistake the porch for the house. If a man would understand himself and discover his resources and put his hand on all life's highest uses, he must look out and up unto his God. Then he comes to know that sunrise and sunset, and the beauty of the earth, and child-life and old age, and duty and sorrow, and all else that life holds, are linked to the larger life of an eternal world.

That is the true foresight. They called him a far-seeing man. How did he get that name? Well, he made a fortune. He managed to make use of the ebb and flow of the market, and never once got stranded. He was shrewd and did some good guessing, and now, forsooth, they say he is 'very far-seeing.' But he has not opened his Bible for years, and the fountains of sympathy are dried up in his soul. He can see as far into the money column as most men, but the financial vista is not very satisfying for those who see it best. The Gospel of St. John is a sealed book to him, and that is in God's handwriting and opens the gates of heaven. Far-seeing? Why, the man is in a tiny cell, and he is going blind. 'Mine eyes are ever toward the Lord.' That is the far-sighted man. He can see an ever larger life opening out before him. He can see the glory of the eternal righteousness beneath his daily duties and the wonder of eternal love in the daily fellowships and fulfilments of the brotherhood. This is measuring life by the heavenly measurement. This is the vision we need day by day and at the end of the days. For interest in some things must wane, and life must become less responsive to all that lies about it, and many an earthly link is broken and many an earthly window is darkened, and the old faces and old ways pass, and the thing the old man cherishes is trodden under foot by the impetuous tread of a new generation, and desire fails. Then it is well with him whose eyes have already caught glimpses of 'the King in His beauty,' and 'the land that is very far off.'

But think for a moment of the present value of the divine outlook upon life. It brings guidance and deliverance. Set side by side the two expressions 'eyes unto the Lord,' and 'feet out of the net.' Life is more than a vision; it is a pilgrimage. We see the far white peaks whereon rests the glory of life, but reaching them is not a matter of eyes, but of feet. Here, maybe, the real problem of godly living presents itself to us. Here our Christian idealism lays a burden on us. It is possible to see distances that would take days to traverse. Even so we can see heights of spiritual possibility that we shall not reach while the light holds good unless we foot it bravely. And it is not an easy journey. There are so many snares set for the pilgrims of faith and hope. There are subtle silken nets woven of soft-spun deceits and filmy threads of sin; and there are coarse strong nets fashioned by the strong hands of passion and evil desire. There are nets of doubt and pain and weakness. But think of the man whose eyes were ever towards the Lord. He came through all right. He always does. He always will. He looked steadily upward to his God. When we get into the net we yield to the natural tendency to look down at our feet. We try to discover how the net is made. We delude ourselves with the idea that if only we take time we shall be able to extricate ourselves; but it always means getting further entangled. It is a waste of time to study the net. Life is ever weaving for us snares too intricate for us to unravel and too strong for us to break. God alone understands how they are made and how they may be broken. He does not take us round the net or over it, but He does not leave us fast by the feet in the midst of it. He always brings a man out on the heavenward side of the earthly difficulty. Look upward and you are bound to go forward.

V.

THE SAFEGUARDED SOUL

The Lord shall keep thee from all evil;
He shall keep thy soul.

Ps. cxxi. 7.

One of the great offices of religion is to help men to begin at the beginning. If you wish to straighten out a tangle of string, you know that it is worth your while to look patiently for one of the ends. If you make an aimless dash at it the result is confusion worse confounded, and by-and-by the tangle is thrown down in despair, its worst knots made by the hands that tried in a haphazard way to simplify it. Life is that tangle; and religion, if it does not loosen all the knots and straighten all the twists, at least shows us where the two ends are. They are with God and the soul. God deals with a man's soul. We cannot explain the facts of our experience or the fashion of our circumstance save in as far as we can see these things reflected in our character. The true spiritual philosophy of life begins its inquiry in the soul, and works outward into all the puzzling mass of life's details. And the foundation of such a philosophy is not experience, but faith. It is true that experience often confirms faith, but faith interprets experience. Experience asks more questions than it can answer. It collects more facts than it can explain. It admits of many different constructions being put upon it. It puts us first of all into touch with the problem of life rather than the solution. If the gentle, patient words of the saint are the utterance of one who has suffered, so also are the bitter protests of the disappointed worldling. The fashion of the experience may be the same in each case. It is faith that makes the lesson different. It is a want of faith that makes us expect the lower in life to explain the higher, the outward to shed light upon the inward. We pluck with foolish, aimless fingers at this strange tangle of human life. We judge God's way with us as far as we can see it, and we think we have got to the end of it. We draw our shallow conclusions. Faith teaches us that God's way with us is a longer and a deeper way, and the end of that way is down in the depths of our spirit, hidden in the love of our character. It is not here and now. It is in what we shall be if God have His will with us.

All the true definitions of things are written in the soul. It was here that the Psalmist found his definition of evil. 'The Lord shall keep thee from all evil; He shall keep thy soul.' Then evil is something that threatens the soul. It is not material, but spiritual. It is not in our circumstances themselves, but in their effect upon the inward life. The same outward conditions of life may be good or evil according to their influence on our character. Good and evil are not qualities of things. They have no meaning apart from the soul. The world says that health and wealth are good, and that sickness and poverty are evil. If that were true the line that separates the healthy from the sick, the rich from the poor, would also separate the happy from the miserable. But we find joy and sorrow on both sides of that line. We are drawn to look deeper than this for our definition of good and evil. We have to make the soul the final arbiter amid these conflicting voices. Here we must find the true definition of evil. The first question we ask when we hear of a house having been burnt down is this: 'Was there any loss of life?' All else lies on a vastly lower plane of interest and importance. So must we learn to distinguish between the house of circumstance, or the house of the body, and the soul that dwells in it. The only real loss is the 'loss of life,' the loss of any of these inner things that go to make the soul's strength and treasure. The man who has lost everything except faith and hope has, maybe, lost nothing at all. There are some among the pilgrims of faith to-day who would never have been found there had not God cast upon their shoulders the ragged cloak of poverty; and if you know anything about that band of pilgrims you will know that the man who outstrips his companions is often a man who is lame on both his feet.

O sceptic world, this is the final answer to your scepticism, an answer none the less true because you cannot receive it: *The Lord keepeth the souls of His saints.* Have you not seen men thinning out a great tree, cutting off some of its noblest branches and marring its splendid symmetry? And very likely you have felt it was a great shame to do so. But that work of maiming and spoiling meant light and sunshine and air in a close and darkened room. It meant health to the dwellers in the house over which the tree had cast its shadow. It is much to have tall and stately trees in the garden of life. But by-and-by that great oak of vigour begins to darken the windows of faith, and God lops some of the branches. We call it suffering, but it means more light. Or it may be that those firs of lordly ambition have grown taller than the roof-tree, and God sends forth His storm-wind to lay them low. We call it failure, but it means a better view of the stars. Ah, yes, we are over-anxious about the trees in the garden. God cares most of all that the light of His truth and the warmth of His love and the breath of His Spirit shall reach and fill every room in the house of life.

He shall keep thy soul. That is a promise that can fold us in divine comfort and peace, and that can do something towards interpreting for us every coil of difficulty, every hour of pain. But if this is to be so, we must ourselves be true to the view of life the promise gives us. We must think of the soul as God thinks of it. We live in a world where souls are cheap. They are bought and sold day by day. It is strange beyond all understanding that the only thing many a man is not afraid of losing is the one thing that is really worth anything to him—his soul. Sometimes the lusts of the world drag down our heart's desire, and we have to confess with shame to moments in our experience when we have not been at all concerned with what became of our soul so long as the desire of the hour was fulfilled or satisfied. We need to seek day by day that the masterful and abiding desires of our heart may be set upon undying good, and that our aspiration may never fold its wings and rest on anything lower than the highest. This shall not make dreamers of us. It shall stand us in good stead in the thick of the world. The man who gets 'the best of the bargain' is always the man who is most honest; for the most precious thing that a man stands to win or lose in any deal is the cleanness of his soul. The man who gets the best of the argument is always the man who is most truthful; for a quiet conscience is better than a silenced opponent. The man who gets the best of life is the man who keeps the honour of his soul; for Jesus said: 'What shall it profit a man if he gain the whole world and lose his own soul?'

So then, amid the manifold uncertainties of human life and the ever-changing forms and complexions of human experience, one thing is pledged beyond all doubt to every man who seeks the will of God and the promise for the safeguarding of his soul. He may write this at the top of every page in the book of life. He may take it for his light in dark days, his comfort in sad days, his treasure in empty days. He may have it on his lips in the hour of battle and in his heart in the day of disappointment. He may meet his temptations with it, interpret his sufferings with it, build his ideal with it. And it shall come to pass that he shall learn to look with untroubled eyes upon the outward things of life, nor fear the touch of its thousand grasping hands, knowing that his soul is in the hands of One who can keep it safe in all the world's despite, even God Himself.

VI.

A PLEA FOR TEARS

They that sow in tears shall reap in joy.
He that goeth forth and weepeth, bearing precious seed,
Shall doubtless come again with rejoicing,
Bringing his sheaves with him.

Ps. cxxvi. 5, 6.

It is almost impossible to recall the joys and sorrows of life without having some thought of their compensative relation. We set our bright days against our dark days. We weigh our successes against our failures. When the hour through which we are living is whispering a bitter message, we recall the kindlier messages of other hours and say that we have much for which we ought to be thankful. And such a deliberate handling of experience, such a quiet adjustment of memories, is not without its uses. Any view of life that will save a man from whining is worth taking. Any reckoning that will prevent a man from indulging in self-pity—that subtlety of selfishness—is worth making. There is, moreover, something very simple and obvious in this way of thinking and judging. To make one kind of experience deal with another kind, to set the days and the hours in battle array—or shall we say to arrange a tourney where some gaily-caparisoned and well-mounted Yesterday is set to tilt with a black-visored and silent To-day—is a way of dealing with life which seems to have much to commend it. But it has at the best serious limitations, and at the worst it may issue in a tragedy. The wrong knight may be unhorsed. The award may go to him of the black plume. Pitting one experience against another has gone to the making of many a cynic and not a few despairing souls. The compensative interpretation of joy and sorrow may bring an answer of peace to a man's soul, or it may not. But in this matter we are deal-

28

ing with things in which we cannot afford to risk an equivocal or a despairing answer. We must win in every encounter. It is not an hour's joy, but a life's outlook that is at stake. No hour's fight was ever worth fighting if it was fought for the sake of the hour. The moments are ever challenging the eternal, the swift and busy hours fling their gauntlets at the feet of the ageless things. The real battle of life is never between yesterday and to-day; it is always between to-day and the Forever.

To isolate an experience is to misinterpret it. We may even completely classify experiences, and yet completely misunderstand experience. To understand life at all we must get beyond the incidental and the alternating. Life is not a series of events charged with elements of contrast, contradiction, or surprise. It is a deep, coherent, and unfaltering process. And one feels that it was something more than the chance of the moment that led the singer of old to weave the tears and the rejoicings of men's lives into a figure of speech that stands for unity of process, even the figure of the harvest.

They that sow in tears shall reap in joy. The sweep of golden grain is not some arbitrary compensation for the life of the seed cast so lavishly into the ground, and biding the test of darkness and cold. It is the very seed itself fulfilled of all its being. Even so it is with the sorrows of these hearts of ours and the joy unto which God bringeth us. He does not fling us a few glad hours to atone for the hours wherein we have suffered adversity. There is a deep sense in which the joys of life are its ripened sorrows.

They that sow in tears…. He that goeth forth and weepeth. These are not the few who have been haunted by apparent failure, or beset with outwardly painful conditions of service. They are not those who have walked in the shadow of a lost leader, or toiled in the grey loneliness of a lost comrade or of a brother proved untrue. For apparent failure, outward difficulty and loneliness, often as we may have to face them, are, after all, only the accidents of Godward toil. And if the bearer of seed for God's great harvest should go forth to find no experience of these things, still, if he is to do any real work in the fields of the Lord, he must go forth weeping. He must sow in tears. Let a man be utterly faithful and sincere, let him open his heart without reserve to the two great claims of the ideal and sympathy, and he shall come to know that he has not found the hidden meaning of daily service, nor learned how he can best perform that service, until he has tasted the sorrow at the heart of it. The tears that are the pledge of harvest are not called to the eyes by ridicule or opposition. They are not the tears of disappointment, vexation, or impotence. They are tears that dim the eyes of them that see visions, and gather in the heart of them that dream dreams. To see the glory of God in the face of Jesus Christ and the blindness of the world's heart to that glory; to see unveiled the beauty that should be, and, unveiled too, the shame that is; to have a spiritual nature that thrills at the touch of the perfect love and life, and responds to every note of pain borne in upon it from the murmurous trouble of the world,—this is to have inward fitness for the high work of the Kingdom. Yes, and it is the pledge that this work shall be done. There is such a thing as artistic grief. There is the vain and languorous pity of aestheticism. Its robe of sympathy is wrapped about itself and bejewelled with its own tears. And it never goes forth. You never meet it in 'the darkness of the terrible streets.'

He that goeth forth and weepeth. It is his tears that cause him to go forth. It is his sorrow that will not let him rest. True pity is a mighty motive. When the real abiding pathos of life has gripped a man's heart, you will find him afield doing the work of the Lord. You will not see his tears. There will be a smile in his eyes and, maybe, a song on his lips. For the sorrow and the joy of service dwell side by side in a man's life. Indeed, they often seem to him to be but one thing. It were a mistake to refer the whole meaning of the words about a man's coming 'again with rejoicing, bringing his sheaves with him' to some far day when the reapers of God shall gather the last great harvest of the world. Through his tears the sower sees the harvest. Through all his life there rings many a sweet prophetic echo of the harvest home.

He that goeth forth and weepeth. No man ever wept like that and went not forth, but some go forth who have not wept. And they go forth to certain failure. They mishandle life, and with good intent do harm. But that is not the worst thing to be said about these toilers without tears. It is not that they touch life so unskilfully, but they touch so little of it. It is only through his tears that a man sees what his work is and where it lies. Tearless eyes are purblind. We have yet much to learn about the real needs of the world. So many try very earnestly to deal with situations they have never yet really seen. For the uplifting of men and for the great social task of this our day we need ideas, and enthusiasm, and all sorts of resource; but most of all, and first of all, we need vision. And the man who goes farthest, and sees most, and does most, is 'he that goeth forth and weepeth.'

VII.

DELIVERANCE WITH HONOUR

He shall call upon Me, and I will answer him;
I will be with him in trouble:
I will deliver him, and honour him.
With long life will I satisfy him,
And show him My salvation.

Ps. xci. 15, 16.

He shall call upon Me. He shall need Me. He shall not be able to
live without Me. As the years pass over his head he shall learn that
there is one need woven into human life larger and deeper and
more abiding than any other need—and that need is God. Thus
doth divinity prophesy concerning humanity. Thus doth infinite
foresight predict a man's need.

We peer in our purblind fashion into the future and try to antici-
pate our needs. We fence ourselves in with all sorts of fancied secu-
rities, and then we comfort ourselves with the shrewdness and
completeness of our forecasting and provision-making. And sometimes it is just folly with a grave face. 'He shall call upon Me.' A man
has learned nothing until he has learned that he needs God. And we
take a long time over that lesson. It has sometimes to be beaten into
us—written in conscience and heart by the finger of pain. How the
little storehouse of life has to be almost stripped of its treasures,
how our faith in the things of the hour has to be played with and
mocked, ere we call upon God in heaven to fill us with abiding
treasure and fold us in eternal love.

He shall call upon Me, and, I will answer him. But I have called, says
one, and He has not answered. I called upon Him when my little
child was sick unto death, and, spite my calling, the little white soul

32

fluttered noiselessly into the great beyond. My friend, you call that tiny green mound in the churchyard God's silence. Some day you will call it God's answer. Our prayers are sometimes torn out of our hearts by the pain of the moment. God's answers come forth from the unerring quiet of eternity. 'He shall call upon Me.' 'He shall ask Me to help him, but he does not know how he can be helped. He is hedged about by a thousand limitations of thought. His life is full of distortions. He cannot distinguish between a blessing and a curse. I cannot heed the dictations of his prayers, but I will answer him.' This is the voice of Him to whom the ravelled complexities of men's minds are simplicity itself; who dwells beyond the brief bewilderments and mistaken desirings and false ideals of men's hearts.

Oh these divine answers! How they confuse us! It is their perfection that bewilders us; it is their completeness that carries them beyond our comprehension.

There is the stamp of the local and the temporary on all our asking. The answer that comes is wider than life and longer than time, and fashioned after a completeness whereof we do not even dream.

I will be with him in trouble. Trouble is that in life which becomes to us a gospel of tears, a ministry of futility. This is because we have grasped the humanity of the word and missed the divinity of it. We are always doing that. Always gathering the meaning of the moments and missing the meaning of the years. Always smarting under the sharp discipline and missing the merciful design: 'With Him in trouble.' That helps me to believe in my religion. Trouble is the test of the creeds. A fig for the orthodoxy that cannot interpret tears! Write vanity upon the religion that is of no avail in the house of sorrow. When the earthly song falls on silence we are disposed to call it a pitiable silence. Not so. Let us say a divinely opportune silence, for when the many voices grow dumb the One Voice speaks: 'I will be with him in trouble,' and the man who has lost the everything that is nothing only to find the one thing that is all knows what that promise means.

I will deliver him. What a masterful, availing, victorious presence is this! How this promise goes out beyond our human ministries of consolation! How often the most we can do is to walk by our brother's side whilst he bears a burden we cannot share! How often the earthly sympathy is just a communion of sad hearts—one weak hand holding another! 'I will deliver him.' That is not merely sympathy, it is victory. The divine love does not merely condole, it delivers.

You cannot add anything to this promise. It is complete. The time of the deliverance is there, the manner of it is there, the whole ministry of help is there. You say you cannot find anything about time and manner. You can only find the bare promise of deliverance. My friend, there are no bare promises in the lips of the Heavenly Father. In the mighty, merciful leisure of omnipotence, in the perfect fitness of things, in a way wiser than his thinking and better than his hoping and larger than his prayer, 'I will deliver him.'

And honour him. It will be no scanty, obscure, uncertain deliverance. There shall be light in it, glory in it. The world battles with its troubles and seems sometimes to be successful, until we see how those troubles have shaken its spirit and twisted its temper; and see, too, how much of the beautiful and the strong and the sweet has been lost in the fight. 'I will deliver him' with an abundant and an honourable deliverance—he shall come forth from his tribulations more noble, tender, and self-possessed. Hereafter there shall be given him the honour of one whom the stress of life has driven into the arms of God.

Oh how we miss this ministry of ennoblement! We reap a harvest of insignificance from the seeds of sorrow sown in our hearts. We let our cares dishonour us. The little cares rasp and fret and sting the manliness and the womanliness and the godlikeness out of us. And the great cares crush us earthward till there is scarcely a sweet word left in our lips or a noble thought in our heart. A man cannot save his *soul* in the day of trouble. He cannot by himself make good the wear and tear of anxieties and griefs. He can hold his head high and hide his secret deep, but he cannot keep his life sweet. Only Christ can teach a man how to find the nameless dignity of the crown of thorns. The kingship of suffering is a secret in the keeping of faith and love. If a man accepts this deliverance of his God folded in flashes of understanding, ministries of explanation, revivals of faith, and gifts of endurance, he shall find the honour that is to be won among life's hard and bitter things.

With long life will I satisfy him, and show him My salvation. We have seen a grey-headed libertine, and we have missed from among the clean-hearted and the faithful some brave young life that was giving itself vigorously to the holy service. But perhaps we have had the grace not to challenge the utter faithfulness of God. The measure of life is not written on a registrar's certificates of birth and death. There is something here that lies beyond dates and documents. Life here and hereafter is one, and death is but an event in it. Who lives to God lives long, be his years many or few. It is reasonable to expect some relationship between godliness and longevity. But we are nearer the truth when we see how that faith and prayer discover and secure the eternal values of fleeting days.

And show him My salvation. That is the whole text summed up in one phrase. That is the life of the godly man gathered into the compass of the divine promise. For every one who goes the way of faith and obedience, life in every phase of it, life here and hereafter, means but one thing and holds but one thing, and that is *the salvation of the Lord*.

VIII.

PETITION AND COMMUNION

Hear me speedily, O Lord....
Cause me to hear ...
For I lift up my soul unto Thee.

Ps. cxliii. 7, 8.

You will notice that the first verse begins 'Hear me,' and the second begins 'Cause me to hear'; and the second is greater than the first. Let us look, then, at these two attitudes of a man in his hour of prayer.

Hear me. The Psalmist began, where all men must begin, with himself. He had something to utter in the hearing of the Almighty. He had something to lay before his God — a story, a confession, a plea. His heart was full, and must outpour itself into the ear of Heaven. 'Hear me speedily, O Lord.' We have all prayed thus. We have all faced some situation that struck a note of urgency in our life, and all your soul has come to our lips in this one cry that went up to the Father, 'Hear me.' A sudden pain, a surprise of sorrow, a few moments of misty uncertainty in the face of decisions that had to be made at once, times when life has tried to rush us from our established position and to bear us we know not where — and our soul has reached out after God as simply and naturally as a man grasps at some fixed thing when he is falling.

There are times, too, when prayer is an indefinable relief. We all know something about the relief of speech. We must speak to somebody. Our need is not, first of all, either advice or practical help. We want a hearing. We want some one to listen and sympathize. We want to share our pain. That is what 'Hear me' sometimes means. Whatever Thou shalt see fit to do for me, at least listen to my cry. Let me unburden my soul. Let me get this weight of silence off my heart. This fashion of relief is part of the true office of prayer. Herein lies the reasonableness of telling our story in the ear of One who knows that story better than we do. We need not inform the All-knowing, but we must commune with the All-pitiful. We make our life known unto God that we may make it bearable unto ourselves.

But let us look at the attitude of mind and heart revealed in this second position, *Cause me to hear*. Now we are coming to the larger truth about prayer, and the deeper spirit of it. Prayer is not merely claiming a hearing; it is giving a hearing. It is not only speaking to God; it is listening to God. And as the heavens are higher than the earth, so are the words we hear greater than the words we speak. Let us not forget this. Let us not pauperize ourselves by our very importunity. Maybe we are vociferous when God is but waiting for a silence to fall in His earthly temples that He may have speech with His children. We talk about 'prevailing prayer,' and there is a great truth in the phrase. All prayer does not prevail. There is that among men which passes for prayer but has no spiritual grip, no assurance, no masterful patience, no fine desperation. There is a place for all these things, and a need for them, in the life of prayer. We need the courage of a great faith and the earnestness that is born of necessity. We need to be able to lift up our faces toward heaven in the swelling joys and the startling perils of these mortal hours and cry, 'Hear me,' knowing that God does hear us and that the outcrying of every praying heart rings clear and strong in the courts of the Heavenly King. But we need something more; we need a very great deal more than this, if we are to enter into the true meaning of prevailing prayer. The final triumph of prayer is not ours; it is God's. When we are upon our knees before Him, it is He, and not we, that must prevail. This is the true victory of faith and prayer, when the Father writes His purpose more clearly in our minds, lays His commandment more inwardly upon our hearts. We do not get one faint glimpse into the meaning of that mysterious conflict at Peniel until we see that the necessity for the conflict lay in the heart of Jacob and not in the heart of God. The man who wrestled with the Angel and prevailed passes before us in the glow of the sunrise weary and halt, with a changed name and a changed heart. So must it be with us; so shall it be, if ever we know what it is to prevail in prayer. Importunity must not become a blind and uninspired clamouring for the thing we desire. Such an attitude may easily set us beyond the possibility of receiving that which God knows we need. We must not forget that our poor little plea for help and blessing does not exhaust the possibilities of prayer. Our words go upward to God's throne twisted by our imperfect thinking, narrowed by our outlook, sterilized by the doubts of our hearts, and we do not know what is good for us. His word comes downward into our lives laden with the quiet certainty of the Eternal, wide as the vision of Him who seeth all, deep as the wisdom of Him who knoweth all.

So, however much it may be to say 'Hear me,' it is vastly more to say 'Cause me to hear.' However much I have to tell Him, He has more to tell me. This view of prayer will help to clear up for us some of the difficulties that have troubled many minds. We hear people speak of unanswered prayer; but there is no such thing, and in the nature of things there cannot be. I do not mean by that, that to every prayer there will come a response some day. To every prayer there is a response now. In our confused and mechanical conception of the God to whom we pray, we separate between His hearing and His answering. We identify the answer to prayer with the granting of a petition. But prayer is more than petition. It is not our many requests, it is an attitude of spirit. We grant readily that our words are the least important part of our prayers. But very often the petitions we frame and utter are no part of our prayers at all. They are not prayer, yet uttering them we may pray a prayer that shall be heard and answered, for every man who truly desires in prayer the help of God for his life receives that help there and then, though the terms in which he describes his need may be wholly wide of the truth as God knows it. So the real answer to prayer is God's response to man's spiritual attitude, and that response is as complete and continuous as the attitude will allow it to be. The end of prayer is not to win concessions from Almighty Power, but to have communion with Almighty Love.

'Cause me to hear'; make a reverent, responsive, receptive silence in my heart, take me out beyond my pleadings into the limitless visions and the fathomless satisfactions of communion with Thyself. Speak to me. That is true prayer.

In the quietness of life,
When the flowers have shut their eye,
And a stainless breadth of sky
Bends above the hill of strife,
Then, my God, my chiefest Good,
Breathe upon my lonelihood:
Let the shining silence be
Filled with Thee, my God, with Thee.

IX.

HAUNTED HOURS

> Wherefore should I fear in the days of evil, when iniquity at
> my heels compasseth me about?

Ps. xlix. 5.

Iniquity *at my heels*. Temptation is very often indirect. It is compact of wiles and subtleties and stratagems. It is adept at taking cover. It does not make a frontal attack unless the obvious state of the soul's defences justifies such a method of attempting a conquest. The stronger a man is, the more subtle and difficult are the ways of sin, as it seeks to enter and to master his life. There are many temptations that never face us, and never give us a chance of facing them. They follow us. We can hear their light footfall and their soft whisperings, but the moment we turn round upon them they vanish. If they disappeared for good, they would be the easiest to deal with of all the ill things that beset our lives. But they do not. The moment we relax our bold, stern search for the face of the enemy, there the evil thing is again—the light footfall and the soft voice. It is terrible work fighting a suggestion. There are the thoughts that a man will not cherish and cannot slay. They may never enter the programme of his life, but there they are, haunting him, waiting, so to speak, at the back of his brain, till he gets used to them. When he seeks to grapple with these enemies his hands close on emptiness. One straight blow, one decisive denial, one stern rebuke, one defiant confession of faith will not suffice for these things. They compass a man's heels. He cannot trample them down. The fashion of the evils that compass us determines the form of the fight we wage with them. Preparations that might amply suffice the city in the day when an army with banners comes against it are no good at all if a plague has to be fought. So there is a way we have to take with 'the iniquity at our heels.' It calls for much patience and much prayer. If we cannot prevent sin from following us, we can at least prevent ourselves from turning and following it. A man can always choose his path if he cannot at every moment determine his company. And as a man goes onward and upward steadfastly toward the City of Light, the evil things fall off and drop behind, and God shall bring him where no evil thing dare follow, and where no ravenous beast shall stalk its prey.

The battle with sin is not an incident in the Christian life; it is the abiding condition of it. While there are some temptations that we have to slay, there are others we have to outgrow. They are overcome, not by any one supreme assertion of the will, but by the patient cultivation of all the loftiest and most wholesome and delicate and intensely spiritual modes of feeling and of being.

Again, let me suggest that iniquity at our heels is sometimes an old sin in a new form. You remember the difficulty that Hiawatha had in hunting down Pau-puk Keewis. That mischievous magician assumed the form of a beaver, then that of a bird, then that of a serpent; and though each in turn was slain, the magician escaped and mocked his pursuer. Surely a parable of our strife with sin. We smite it in one form and it comes to life in another. One day a man is angry — clenched fingers and hot words. He conquers his anger; but the next day there is a spirit of bitterness rankling in his heart, and maybe a tinge of regret that he did not say and do more when his heart was hot within him and fire was on his lips. The sin he faced and fought yesterday has become iniquity at his heels. Having failed to knock him down, it tries to trip him up. Maybe many waste their energies trying to deal with the *forms* of sin, and never grapple with the *fact* of sin. Hence the evil things that compass men's souls about with their dread ministries of suggestion, and flutter on unhallowed wings in the wake of life. The sin that confronts us reveals to us our need of strength, but the sin that dogs our steps has, maybe, a deeper lesson to teach us — even our need of heart-deep holiness. Good resolution will do much to clear the path ahead, but only purity of character can rid us of the persistent haunting peril of the sin that plucks at the skirt of life. The deliverance God offers to the struggling soul covers not only the hour of actual grappling with the foe, but all the hours when it is the stealth and not the strength of evil that we most have cause to fear.

Iniquity at my heels. These words remind us that sin is not done with after it is committed. God forgives sin, but He does not obliterate all its consequences, either in our own lives or in the lives of others. A man may have the light of the City of God flashing in his face, and a whole host of shameful memories and bitter regrets crowding at his heels. We do not know what sin is till we turn our backs on it. Then we find its tenacity and its entanglement. What would we not give if only we could leave some things behind us! What would we not do if only we could put a space between ourselves and our past! The fetters of evil habit may be broken, but their marks are upon us, and the feet that bore the fetters go more slowly for them many days. The hands that have been used to grasping and holding do not open without an effort, even though the heart has at last learned that it is more blessed to give than to receive.

Yes, and our sins come to life again in the lives of others. The light word that ought to have been a grave word and that shook another's good resolution, the cool word that ought to have been a warm word and that chilled a pure enthusiasm — we cannot have done with these things. Parents sometimes live to see their sins of indulgence or of neglect blighting the lives of those to whom they owed a debt of firmness and kindness. It is iniquity at the heels. These passages of carelessness and unfaithfulness haunt men, be their repentance never so bitter and their amendment never so sincere and successful. But all this is for discipline and not for despair. It casts us back upon God's mercy. It keeps the shadow of the cross upon all our path. It has something to do with the making of 'a humble, lowly, penitent, and obedient heart.' The memory of the irreparable is a sorrow of the saints.

Saint, did I say? With your remembered faces,
  Dear men and women whom I sought and slew!
Ah, when we mingle in the heavenly places,
  How will I weep to Stephen and to you!

Only let us not be afraid nor wholly cast down. Rather let us say, 'Wherefore should I fear when the iniquity at my heels compasseth me about?' By the grace of God the hours of the soul's sad memory and of clinging regrets shall mean unto us a ministry of humility and a passion of prayer. And through them God shall give us glimpses of the gateway of that life where regret and shame and sorrow fall back unable to enter. There is a place whither the iniquity at a man's heels can no longer follow him, and where in the perfect life the soul, at last, is able to forget.

X.

THE WINGS OF THE DOVE

And I said, Oh that I had wings like a dove!
Then would I fly away, and be at rest....
I would haste me to a shelter
From the stormy wind and tempest.

Ps. lv. 6, 8.

These words are the transcript of a mood. The writer is not unfolding to us any of the deep persistent longings of his spirit; he is telling us of a thought that shadowed his soul for an hour. Let us look into this mood of his. It is not his in any unique or even peculiar sense. In moods, as in manners, history is wont to repeat itself. The writer of this poem has voiced one of the great common experiences of humanity. But let us be quite clear as to what that experience really is. Let us not be misled by the music and the seeming unworldliness of these words about winged flight from a world of trouble and strife. The Psalmist was not looking heavenward, but earthward, when this plea for wings broke from his heart. He was moved to speak as he did, not by the surpassing charm of a heavenly vision, but by the dark unrest of the earthly outlook. The emphatic note here is that of departure, not of destination. It is necessary to remind ourselves that this is so, for these words have become the classic of the home-sick soul. They have been used to voice the farthest and most truly divine desires of the human heart. And by virtue of such use they have gathered a meaning which was not theirs at the beginning. At that meaning we will presently look, but let us first of all look at this longing as it stands in the psalm and as it represents an experience that is threaded through the history of humanity.

Oh that I had wings ... then would I fly away. Here the idea of fleeing away suggests itself as a possible solution of life; and whenever it comes to a man like this it is a source of weakness. It is not a desire to find the joys of heaven; it is a desire to escape the pains of earth. There is no vista, no wistful distance, no long, alluring prospect. The soul is hemmed in by its enemies, crushed down by its burdens, beset on all sides by the frets of the earthly lot; and there comes a vague desire to be out of it all. It is not aspiration, it is evasion. It is not response to the ideal, it is recoil from the actual. It is not the spell of that which shall be that is upon the soul, but the irksomeness or the dreadfulness of that which is. This is a mood that awaits us all. No man faces life as it should be faced, but some can hardly be said to face it at all. Their face is ever turned towards a seductive vision of quietness. The solution of life for them is not in a fight, but in a retreat. Of course we know there is no going back, and no easy deliverance from the burden and the battle, but in the thick of any fight there is a great difference between the man who wants victory and the man who merely wants a cessation of hostilities.

This plea for wings does not necessarily betoken 'a desire to depart.' It rather indicates a desire to remain under more favourable and comfortable conditions. Such a mood is not the highest and the healthiest experience of the soul. It is rather something against which we must fight relentlessly. Very often the longing for wings results only in lagging footsteps. Picturing to ourselves the luxury of laying life down will not help us to face the duty of taking life up. The secret of enervation is found not in the poverty of our resources, but in the cowardliness and selfishness of our attitude towards life. The battle is half won when we have looked the enemy in the face. The burden is the better borne as we stoop under the full weight of it.

Oh that I had wings like a dove! That is a short-sighted and a selfish desire. Supposing you had wings, what would you do? Fly away from the moil of the world and find rest and shelter for yourself? Is that the best and noblest thing to desire to do? After all, we know other and loftier moods than this. We know that staying is better than going when there is so much to stay for. We know that working is better than resting when there is so much to do. We have something better to think about than a quiet lodgement in the wilderness, we who live in a world where the strength of our hands and the warmth of our hearts count for something. To give your tired brother a lift is a vastly more profitable occupation than sitting at the roadside and wishing you could fly. Man, you ought to be glad that you can walk—in a world where there are so many cripples that want help.

Oh that I had wings!… then would I fly away. That desire has never taken any one to heaven, but it has made them less useful upon earth. The breath of this desire is able to blight the flowers of social service. No one would be foolish enough to indict suburbanism as a mode of life. The day must surely come when few or none will dwell in the smoke-grimed heart of the city. But in as far as a man seeks the fairest suburb open to him in order that he may see little of, and think little of, 'the darkness of the terrible streets,' then the very life that restores health to his body shall sow seeds of disease in his soul.

There is only one way to rest, and that lies right through the heart of the world's work and pain. Rest is not for those who flee away from life's difficulties, but for those who face them. 'Take my yoke … and ye shall find rest.' It were not well for our own sakes that we had wings. It were not well for us to be able to avoid the burden-bearing and the tale of tired days, for God has hidden the secret of our rest in the heart of our toiling. They who come unto the City of God come there not by the easy flight of a dove, but by the long, slow pilgrimage of unselfishness.

Yet there is a beauty and a fitness in this longing. It is expressive of more than the weariness of a world-worn spirit, or the thinly disguised selfishness of one who fears to pay the price of life.

When the long working-day of life is wearing away its last hours and verging towards the great stillness, the voices of time fall but faintly on the ear, the adorations and ideals and fashions and enthusiasms of the world come to mean little to a man who in his day has followed them as eagerly as any, and the heart within him asks only for rest.

God, if there be none beside Thee
  Dwelling in the light,
Take me out of the world and hide me

Somewhere behind the night.

When, like Simeon the seer with the Christ-Child in his arms, a man feels that for him life has said its last word and shown its last wonder and uttered its last benediction, the desire for rest is a pure and spiritually normal thing; it is just the soul's gaze turned upward where

> beyond these toils
> God waiteth us above,
> To give to hand and heart the spoils
> Of labour and of love.

And maybe this mood of which we are thinking may have a not unworthy place in a strenuous life. As a tired woman pauses amid her tasks and looks out of her cottage window to take into her heart the quiet beauty of the woods where she knows the ground is fair with lilies, so do we find ourselves looking out of life's small casement and thinking upon the fresh, free, 'outdoor' life the soul will some day live. And such a mood as this is surely a sign of the soul's growth, a testimony of its responsiveness to the divine touch, a sudden sense of its splendid destiny borne in upon it among the grey and narrow circumstances of its service.

> Oh that I had a dove's swift, silver wings,
> I said, so I might straightway leave behind
> This strife of tongues, this tramp of feet, and find
> A world that knows no struggles and no stings,
> Where all about the soul soft Silence flings
> Her filmy garment, and the vexèd mind
> Grows quiet as there floats upon the wind
> The soothing slumber-song of dreamless things.
> And lo! there answered me a voice and said,
> Man, thou hast hands and heart, take back thy prayer;
> Covet life's weariness, go forth and share
> The common suffering and the toil for bread.
> Look not on Rest, although her face be fair,
> And her white hands shall smooth thy narrow bed.

XI.

A NEW SONG

O sing unto the Lord a new song.

Ps. xcvi. 1.

Time and again in the Psalter we find this appeal for a new song. First of all, and most obviously, the appeal concerns the contents of the song. It reminds us of the duty of making our grateful acknowledgement of God's goodness to us expand with our growing experience of that goodness. It is, if, one may so phrase it, a reminder to us that our praise needs bringing up to date. A hymn considerably later in date than this psalm exhorts us to 'count' our 'blessings,' and to 'name them one by one.' This exhortation to attempt the impossible is perhaps more worthy of being heeded than the form in which it is presented to us might lead some to suppose. There is no getting away from the simple fact that a man's thankfulness has a real and proportionate relationship to the things for which he has cause to be thankful. If in our daily life the phrase 'the goodness of God' is to have a deepening and cumulative significance, it must be informed and vitalized continually by an alert and responsive recognition of the forms in which that goodness is ever freshly manifested to us. Whilst the roots of the tree of praise lie deep beneath the surface, and wind their thousand ways into dim places where memory itself cannot follow them, yet surely the leaves of the tree are fresher and greener for rain that even now has left its reviving touch upon them, and for the sunshine that is even now stirring the life in all their veins. The figure is imperfect. We are not trees. We do not respond automatically to all the gracious and cheering ministries of the Eternal Goodness in our lives. We may easily overlook many a good gift of our God. And though in our forgetfulness and unthankfulness we profit by the sunlight and the dew and by each tender thought of God for His creatures, yet the full and perpetual profit of all good things is for each of us bound up with the power to see them, the wisdom to appraise them, the mindfulness that holds them fast, and the heart that sings out its thanksgiving for them. 'O sing unto the Lord a new song.' Bring this day's life into the song. Bring the gift that has come to thee this very hour into the song. Look about thee. See if there be but one more flower springing at the path-side. See if the bud of yesterday has but unfolded another leaf. Behold the loaf on thy table, feel the warmth of thy hearth, yea, feel the very life within thee that woke again and stirred itself with the morning light, and say these gifts are like unto the gifts of yesterday, but they are not yesterday's gifts. Yesterday's bread is broken, and yesterday's fire is dead, and yesterday's strength is spent. O God, Thy mercies are new every morning! So shall a new song break from the heart.

It is quite possible, in taking what we believe to be a broad view of life, to overlook many of the things that go to make life. Too much generalizing makes for a barren heart. The specific has a vital place in the ministry of praise. It is true that the highest flights of praise always carry the soul beyond any conscious reckoning with the details of its experience. Tabulation is not the keystone of the arch of thanksgiving. But to behold the specific goodness of God in each day's life, to review the hours and to say to one's own soul, Thus and thus hath my God been mindful of me, is perhaps the surest and the simplest way to deepen and vitalize the habit of praise in our life, and to set the new notes ringing in our psalm of thanksgiving.

But in this appeal for a new song of praise to God there is something more than a recognition of new blessings. The new song is not merely the response to new mercies and the tuneful celebration of recent good. If there is to be ever a new note in the song, there must be ever a new note in the singer's heart. And this cometh not by observation, but by inspiration. You may change the words of the song and it may still be the old song. You may sing the same words and it may yet be a new song. For as is the singer, so is the song.

O sing unto the Lord a new song. That is a plea for a deeper and a wider life. It is a plea that sounds the depth of the heart and takes the measure of the soul. The new song comes not of a truer enumeration of life's blessings, but of a truer understanding of the blessedness of life itself. The key to such understanding is character. When by the grace of the clean heart and the enlightened and responsive spirit a man can get beneath the events of each day's life and commune with that eternal law of love to which each one of those events bears some relation—or had we not better say commune with the Eternal Father by whom that law exists?—then is his song of praise ever new. It is something to catch a glimpse of the mercy of God, and to think and feel as one has not thought or felt before about some part of life's daily good. But it is vastly more to learn to interpret the whole of life in the terms of the goodness of God. The saint sings where the worldling sighs. And if we find in that song only the apotheosis of courage and resignation, we have neither found the source of the song nor the message of it. The new song comes not from the thrill of peril faced and defied, nor from the victorious acceptance of hard and bitter things. It comes from that deep life of the soul in God, a life beyond the threat of peril and beyond the touch of pain. It finds its deepest and freshest notes not in contemplating the new gains and good of any day, but in a growing sense of the timeless gain and eternal good of every day.

And if all this be so, it surely follows that the service of praise is not something unto which we may pass by one effort of the will or that depends upon the stimulus of outward experience. It is conditioned rather by our character, and by our power to see the unveiled face of life reflecting always the light of perfect love. And it is to produce in us the right character and the true insight that God disciplines us all our days. It is to set a new song in our hearts. Said a professor of music at Leipzig of a girl whom he had trained for some years and who was the pride of the Conservatoire, 'If only some one would marry her and ill-treat her and break her heart she would be the finest singer in Europe.' He missed something in the song, and knew it could never come there save from the heart of the singer. Trouble always strikes a new note in life, and often the deepest note that is ever struck. But, be our experience joyous or sorrowful, the true end of it must ever be to deepen our own hearts that there may be in us ever a more catholic recognition of, and response to, the Eternal Love.

The human soul is not a mere repository of experiences. Memory is not the true guardian of life's treasure. That treasure is invested in character. In the moral world we *have* what we *are*. So we may recall that which we have never possessed, and may possess that which we can never recall. And it is out of that which we have *become* by God's grace, rather than out of that which we have received of that grace, that the new song comes.

So, as day by day we pray for the grace of new thanksgiving, we are seeking something more than a new power to behold what good things each day brings us, a readier way of reckoning the wealth of the passing hours. We are seeking for a larger life in God, and for a spirit able, as it were, to secrete from every experience its hidden meed of everlasting blessing. For if the heart grow purer, the will stronger, the vision clearer, the judgement truer—indeed, if there come to the soul each day some increase of life—it shall surely find its way into living praise. And a living song is always a new song.